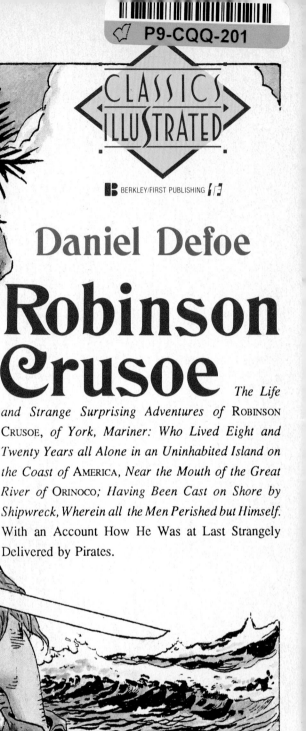

CLASSICS ILLUSTRATED

BERKLEY/FIRST PUBLISHING

Daniel Defoe

Robinson Crusoe

The Life and Strange Surprising Adventures of ROBINSON CRUSOE, *of York, Mariner: Who Lived Eight and Twenty Years all Alone in an Uninhabited Island on the Coast of* AMERICA, *Near the Mouth of the Great River of* ORINOCO; *Having Been Cast on Shore by Shipwreck, Wherein all the Men Perished but Himself. With an Account How He Was at Last Strangely Delivered by Pirates.*

adapted by

Sam Wray
writer

Pat Boyette
artist

Gary Fields
letterer

Bill Wray
cover artist

Robinson Crusoe, Daniel Defoe's compelling tale of the shipwrecked sailor who spent 28 years on a deserted island, was based on a true story. Alexander Selkirk, a young Scottish seaman of foul temper who was prone to fits of violence, had requested to be put ashore on an uninhabited island in 1704 following an argument with the master of his ship. After an initial eight-month period of desperate loneliness, he accepted his lot and made a life, such as it was, on his island prison. Selkirk was rescued in 1709, nearly inarticulate but otherwise in good health, and became a celebrity when he returned home. Defoe is said to have met the sailor, and his fictionalized account of Selkirk's story was published in 1719, to instant and permanent acclaim. At the time **Robinson Crusoe** was written, Defoe was a fading journalist in his sixties. A political and religious dissenter, he had been fined, imprisoned, and pilloried for publication of *The Shortest Way with Dissenters* (1702), a pamphlet in which he satirically argued for the total, savage suppression of all dissent. He was a prolific writer, and produced 560 books, pamphlets, and tracts — *Moll Flanders* (1722) and *A Tour Thro' the Whole Island of Great Britain* (1724–1726) are among the best of them — but he is most remembered for **Robinson Crusoe**, an almost universally familiar tale. He took the story of Selkirk, a borderline psychotic, and transformed it into an uplifting fable of the healthy, religious, and practical Crusoe. Although considered by some to be a children's story, the real theme is not so much about the plight of a shipwrecked sailor, as it is about a man's mastery of a hostile environment through hard work, tenacity, and faith. As such, it reflects Defoe's position as an outsider in English society and his sense of alienation from its entrenched powers. While the claim that **Crusoe** was the first English novel is open to interpretation, Defoe was certainly the first writer to elevate the novel from a minor accomplishment to a major art form.

Robinson Crusoe
Classics Illustrated, Number 23

Wade Roberts, Editorial Director   Kurt Goldzung, Creative Director
Mike McCormick, Art Director   Valarie Jones, Editor

PRINTING HISTORY
1st edition published April 1991

For information, address: First Publishing, Inc., 435 North LaSalle St., Chicago, Illinois 60610.

ISBN 0-425-12664-1

Distributed by Berkley Sales & Marketing, a division of The Berkley Publishing Group, 200 Madison Avenue, New York, New York 10016.

Printed in the United States of America
1 2 3 4 5 6 7 8 9 0

I WAS BORN IN THE YEAR 1632, IN THE CITY OF YORK, OF GOOD FAMILY AND MIDDLE ESTATE. MY FATHER HAD EDUCATED ME WELL AND DESIGNED ME FOR THE LAW; BUT I WOULD BE SATISFIED WITH NOTHING BUT GOING TO SEA, AND THIS LED ME SO STRONGLY AGAINST THE WILL OF MY PARENTS THAT THERE SEEMED TO BE SOMETHING FATAL IN THAT PROPENSITY.

A FRIEND OFFERED ME FREE PASSAGE TO LONDON ON HIS FATHER'S SHIP. I CONSULTED NEITHER FATHER NOR MOTHER, LEAVING THEM WITHOUT ASKING GOD'S BLESSING OR MY FATHER'S. IN AN ILL HOUR, ON THE FIRST OF SEPTEMBER, 1651, I WENT ON BOARD THE SHIP.

ON THE EIGHTH DAY AT SEA, IT BLEW A FRIGHTFUL STORM. THE SHIP FOUNDERED AND WE HAD TO GET TO SHORE BY BOAT, AND NOT WITHOUT GREAT DIFFICULTY. I THEN SHOULD HAVE GONE HOME, BUT MY BLIND OBSTINACY AGAIN PUSHED ME TOWARD THE SEA.

ON SHORE, I WAS DRIVEN BY THE WILD NOTION OF MAKING A FORTUNE; I JOINED A VESSEL BOUND FOR AFRICA, WHERE WE WOULD TRADE ON THE GUINEA COAST.

IN THAT VOYAGE ONLY, I WAS SUCCESSFUL. I BROUGHT BACK GOLD ENOUGH TO SELL FOR 300 £ IN LONDON. BUT AGAIN MY OBSTINATE LONGINGS URGED ME TO ANOTHER, MOST UNFORTUNATE, VOYAGE...

ON MY SECOND VOYAGE TO THE GUINEA COAST WE WERE SURPRISED BY A TURKISH ROVER. AFTER A GREAT STRUGGLE, THE TURKS CARRIED US, PRISONERS, INTO THE MOORISH PORT OF SALLEE.

I REMAINED TWO YEARS A SLAVE, EVER THINKING OF ESCAPE.

MY CHANCE CAME WHEN MY MASTER SENT ME WITH HIS BOAT TO CATCH FISH, ALONG WITH A MAN AND A BOY FROM HIS HOUSEHOLD. I TOOK THE MAN BY SURPRISE AND THREW HIM INTO THE SEA, AND GOT THE BOY TO JOIN ME IN MY PLAN.

I TOOK OUR BOAT SOUTH. ONE CLEAR DAY, MY HELPER CRIED OUT IN ALARM.

THE CAPTAIN WAS AGREEABLE TO CARRY ME TO THE BRAZILS.

FROM THE SALE OF MY TURKISH FISHING BOAT, I BOUGHT LAND IN BRAZIL, AND LEARNED THE GROWING OF TOBACCO AND THE PRODUCTION OF SUGAR. YET I WAS AGAIN TO BE THE AGENT OF MY OWN MISERIES!

HAVING LIVED ALMOST FOUR YEARS IN BRAZIL, I HAD FREQUENTLY TALKED OF MY SUCCESSFUL TRADING ON THE GUINEA COAST. THIS TALK, TOGETHER WITH OUR NEED FOR LABOR ON THE PLANTATIONS, LED MY ACQUAINTANCES TO MAKE A SECRET PROPOSAL TO ME.

BUT I WAS BORN TO BE MY OWN DESTROYER, AND COULD NO MORE RESIST THE OFFER THAN I COULD RESTRAIN MY RAMBLING DESIGNS. I JOINED THE VOYAGE ON THE FIRST OF SEPTEMBER, 1659.

IT WAS PREPOSTEROUS OF ME TO THINK OF SUCH A VOYAGE AS THEY OFFERED!

WE HAD GOOD WEATHER FOR MORE THAN TWELVE DAYS, BUT THEN A HURRICANE STRUCK US. IT BLEW IN SUCH A TERRIBLE MANNER THAT NONE IN THE SHIP EXPECTED TO SAVE THEIR LIVES!

WE SOUGHT TO STEER FOR THE ENGLISH COLONIES, BUT THE FURIES OF THE STORM DEFEATED US. JUST AS ONE OF OUR MEN CRIED OUT "LAND!" OUR SHIP STRUCK SAND AND THE SEA BROKE OVER HER!

WE COULD NOT SO MUCH AS HOPE, THAT THE SHIP MIGHT HOLD TOGETHER. WE GOT A BOAT OVER THE SIDE. OUR BOAT WAS OVERTURNED AND SWALLOWED INTO THE MONSTROUS FLOOD'

I THOUGHT I COULD SWIM WELL, BUT MY MOST DESPERATE STRUGGLES COULD NOT DELIVER ME SO AS TO DRAW A FULL BREATH OF AIR INTO MY AGONIZED LUNGS.

I WAS HALF DEAD WITH THE WATER I TOOK IN.

I COULD FEEL MYSELF CARRIED WITH A MIGHTY FORCE AND SWIFTNESS, A GREAT WAY.

AFTER MANY DESPERATE RUNS I FINALLY GOT TO THE SHORE, SOBBING FROM EXERTION AND FEAR, BUT ESCAPED FROM THE TERRIBLE EMBRACE OF THE SEA!

I WAS LANDED SAFE ON SHORE; I BEGAN TO THANK GOD THAT MY LIFE WAS SAVED. I LIFTED UP MY HANDS IN THE CONTEMPLATION OF MY DELIVERANCE.

I REFLECTED THAT ALL MY COMRADES WERE DROWNED. I NEVER SAW A SIGN OF THOSE MEN AFTERWARDS EXCEPT FOR THREE OF THEIR HATS, ONE CAP, AND TWO SHOES THAT WERE NOT FELLOWS.

NIGHT COMING UPON ME, I BEGAN WITH HEAVY HEART TO CONSIDER WHAT WOULD BE MY LOT IF THERE WERE ANY RAVENOUS BEASTS IN THAT COUNTRY, FOR AT NIGHT THEY SEEK THEIR PREY.

I HAD NOTHING WITH ME BUT A KNIFE, A PIPE, AND A LITTLE TOBACCO. WITH MY KNIFE I WAS ABLE TO CUT A SHORT STICK, LIKE A TRUNCHEON, FOR MY DEFENSE.

HAVING ALREADY FOUND A SOURCE OF FRESH WATER TO DRINK, I PUT A LITTLE TOBACCO IN MY MOUTH TO PREVENT HUNGER, AND TOOK UP LODGING IN A THICK BUSHY TREE. THERE, EXCESSIVELY FATIGUED, I FELL FAST ASLEEP.

WHEN I WAKED THE STORM HAD ABATED; THE SHIP HAD BEEN DRIVEN WITHIN A MILE FROM THE SHORE. MY GRIEF WAS RENEWED; IF WE HAD STAYED ON BOARD WE ALL WOULD HAVE BEEN SAVED, AND I WOULD NOT BE SO MISERABLY ALONE.

WALKING THE SHORE, THE FIRST THING I FOUND WAS THE BOAT, WHICH LAY AS THE WIND AND SEA HAD TOSSED HER.

I RESOLVED, IF POSSIBLE, TO GET ABOARD THE SHIP, FOR I WAS IN DIRE NEED OF PROVISIONS.

I SWAM AROUND HER TWICE, AND THE SECOND TIME I SPY'D A SMALL LENGTH OF ROPE THAT I MIGHT REACH.

My first act was to find food and drink. Then I looked about; I found the ship damaged at the hull with water in her hold, but she lay with her stern high and her quarter dry.

I wanted a boat to carry provisions to the shore, but having no boat, I tied yards and spars together in the form of a raft.

When my raft was strong enough to bear a reasonable weight, my next care was what I should load it with.

I got three seamen's chests and filled them with provisions: bread, rice, cheeses, dried goat's flesh, and the like. But my greatest prize was the carpenter's chest, at that time more valuable to me than a boat load of gold.

My next care was for ammunition and arms; there were two good fowling pieces and two pistols, as well as powder and shot.

I now thought myself pretty well freighted, and I began to think how I should best get myself to shore with my cargo and the ship's cats.

I HAD THE ENCOURAGEMENT OF A CALM SEA, A RISING TIDE, AND A FAVORABLE BREEZE.

I NEARLY HAD A SECOND SHIPWRECK WHEN MY RAFT GROUNDED UPON A SHOAL!

I DID MY UTMOST, BUT I COULD NOT THRUST OFF THE RAFT, NEITHER DURST I STIR FROM HOLDING UP THE CHESTS...

I HAD STOOD THUS FOR NEAR HALF AN HOUR, BEFORE THE RISING OF THE WATER FREED MY RAFT AGAIN. AND JUST AT THIS TIME, TO MY SURPRISE, FOR I HAD THOUGHT HIM LOST, THE SHIP'S DOG CAME SWIMMING TO SHORE.

I WAITED 'TIL THE TIDE WAS HIGHEST, AND THEN GOT MY RAFT AND CARGO SAFE ON SOLID LAND.

MY NEXT WORK WAS TO VIEW THE COUNTRY AND SEEK A PROPER PLACE FOR MY HABITATION, AND TO LEARN IF THE COUNTRY WAS INHABITED, AND IF THERE WOULD BE ANY DANGER FROM WILD BEASTS.

I WENT FOR DISCOVERY TO A HIGH HILL. I HAD GREAT LABOUR AND DIFFICULTY GETTING TO THE TOP.

I WAS ON AN ISLAND ENVIRONED EVERY WAY WITH THE SEA. NEITHER HERE NOR THERE DID I SEE ANY SIGN OF HUMAN HABITATION. AS FOR WILD BEASTS, I SAW NONE FOR CERTAIN, BUT I THOUGHT I SAW TWO OR THREE GOATS.

I SAW AN ABUNDANCE OF FOWLS, BUT KNEW NOT THEIR KINDS NEITHER COULD I TELL WHICH WAS FIT FOR FOOD AND WHICH NOT.

I SHOT A GREAT BIRD WHICH I SAW SITTING IN A TREE: I TOOK IT TO BE A KIND OF HAWK, BUT IT HAD NO TALONS OR CLAWS MORE THAN COMMON BIRDS. I FOUND ITS FLESH FIT FOR NOTHING.

THE SOUND OF MY SHOT HAD A GREAT EFFECT, AS IF IT WERE THE FIRST GUN THAT HAD BEEN FIRED THERE SINCE THE BEGINNING OF THE WORLD! THERE AROSE INNUMERABLE FOWLS, OF MANY SORTS, SCREAMING AND CRYING, BUT NOT ONE OF THEM WAS OF A KIND THAT I KNEW.

I THOUGHT THAT I MIGHT YET GET A GREAT MANY THINGS OUT OF THE SHIP.

I FOUND A GRINDSTONE, NAILS, SPIKES, IRON CROW-BARS, AND HATCHETS.

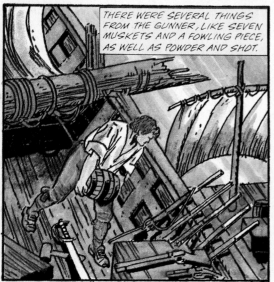

THERE WERE SEVERAL THINGS FROM THE GUNNER, LIKE SEVEN MUSKETS AND A FOWLING PIECE, AS WELL AS POWDER AND SHOT.

I WAS UNDER SOME APPREHENSION THAT MY PROVISIONS ON SHORE MIGHT BE DEVOURED BY ANIMALS PROWLING THERE.

I FIRST LOOKED FOR GARMENTS OF MY SIZE, BUT UPON REFLECTION, I TOOK THEM ALL.

I SPY'D WHAT I HAD MISSED BEFORE: THERE WERE PENS, INK, AND WRITING PAPER. MY THOUGHTS FIXED ON WRITING A JOURNAL, BUT I KNEW I MUST FINISH MY LABOR AT THE SHIP'S PROVISIONS, WHICH WOULD TAKE MANY DAYS.

HA!

I HAD NOW BEEN THIRTEEN DAYS ON SHORE AND ELEVEN TIMES ON THE SHIP.

I BELIEVE, VERILY, HAD THE CALM WEATHER HELD, I SHOULD HAVE BROUGHT AWAY THE WHOLE SHIP, PIECE BY PIECE!

THE TWELFTH TIME GOING ABOARD, I FELT THE WIND BEGIN TO RISE.

I THOUGHT I HAD RUMMAGED THE CABIN EFFECTUALLY, BUT I DISCOVERED YET ANOTHER LOCKER.

I FOUND ABOUT 36 POUNDS VALUE IN COINS OF EUROPE AND BRAZIL.

OH DRUG! WHAT ART THOU GOOD FOR? I HAVE NO MANNER OF USE FOR THEE!

HOWEVER, ON SECOND THOUGHT, I TOOK THE MONEY WITH ME.

11

H AVING SAVED THE PROVISIONS FROM THE SHIP, I HAD NOW TO PROTECT THEM WITH A FENCE.

MY DESIGN WAS A SEMI-CIRCULAR FENCED FIELD ON THE NORTH-NORTH-WEST OF A VERY STEEP HILL.

MY PALING ENCLOSED A PART OF A FLAT PLAIN ABOUT A HUNDRED YARDS WIDE BY TWICE THAT LONG.

THE ENTRANCE I MADE TO BE NOT BY A DOOR, BUT ONLY BY A SHORT LADDER, WHICH I LIFTED AFTER ME WHEN I CROSSED.

I HAD BY NOW STORED MY PROVISIONS IN A SHALLOW CAVE WHICH I HAD MADE IN THE HILL, AND IN FRONT OF THIS I HAD A TENT.

OH, MY GUN-POWDER!

THE THOUGHT DARTED INTO MY MIND, AS SWIFT AS THE LIGHT-NING: AT ONE BLAST MY POWDER MIGHT BE DESTROYED!

I PASSED A MOST MISERABLE NIGHT.

THE STORM WAS OVER, BUT NOT MY ANXIETY.

I LAID ASIDE ALL MY OTHER WORK, TO MAKE BAGS AND BOXES TO SEPARATE THE GUNPOWDER SO AS TO STORE IT IN DIFFERENT PLACES.

HOME IN MY ENCLOSURE, I STAYED WITH ALL MY WEALTH ABOUT ME, VERY SECURE. I HAD SET UP A LARGE POST AND UPON IT I CARVED THE WORDS "I CAME TO SHORE HERE ON THE 30TH OF SEPTEMBER, 1659." UPON THE SIDES OF IT I CUT EVERY DAY BY A NOTCH.

I THOUGHT AS WELL THAT I SHOULD NOW BEGIN TO ORDER MY TIMES OF WORK, OF GOING OUT WITH MY GUN AT AN EARLY HOUR, OF WORKING AT MY CAMP, OF EATING, OF SLEEPING DURING THE HOURS OF EXCESSIVE HEAT, AND OF KEEPING A JOURNAL.

November 5th. I WENT ABROAD WITH MY GUN AND DOG AND KILLED A WILD CAT. HER SKIN WAS PRETTY SOFT, BUT THE FLESH WAS GOOD FOR NOTHING.

Nov. 17. THIS DAY I BEGAN TO DIG BEHIND MY TENT TO MAKE MORE ROOM. I LOOSENED THE EARTH WITH A CROW-BAR, BUT KNOWING I COULD DO LITTLE MORE DIGGING WITHOUT A SHOVEL I THOUGHT TO MAKE ONE OF HARDWOOD FROM THE FOREST.

14

Nov. 18. I FOUND A TREE OF THE SORT THAT IS CALLED IRON-WOOD IN THE BRAZILS. ALMOST SPOILING MY AXE ON ITS HARDNESS, I CUT A LENGTH OF IT AND CARRIED IT HOME, THOUGH IT WAS EXCEEDINGLY HEAVY.

NEVER WAS SO LONG A MAKING OF A SHOVEL; WITH THAT AND THE MAKING OF A SORT OF HOD TO CARRY LOOSE EARTH FROM MY DIGGING, I NEEDED ALL OF FOUR DAYS.

Dec. 10. JUST AS I BEGAN TO THINK OF THE WORK AS NEARLY FINISHED, A GREAT QUANTITY OF EARTH FELL FROM THE TOP AND SIDE OF THE CAVE!

Nov. 23. BEGINNING TO WORK, I WIDENED AND DEEPENED MY CAVE, WHICH I MUCH NEEDED AS A WAREHOUSE, KITCHEN, DINING ROOM AND CELLAR. BUT THERE WERE UNEXPECTED PROBLEMS.

Dec. 11. THIS DAY I GOT POSTS PITCHED TO SECURE THE ROOF. Dec. 17. I PLACED UP SHELVES IN THE CAVE. Dec. 20. I CARRIED EVERYTHING INSIDE, AND MADE A TABLE.

Dec. 31. from Dec. 24. TO THIS DATE THERE WERE LONG RAINS AND DAYS OF GREAT HEAT. I PASSED THE TIME PUTTING MY THINGS IN ORDER. MY THOUGHTS TURNED TO THE IDEA OF BUILDING A SORT OF WALL OR PALING, FOR THE PROTECTION OF MY HABITATION.

Jan. 2. I HAD SUSPECTED THAT THERE WERE GOATS ON MY ISLAND. NOW I ENCOUNTERED THEM.

FOR THE FIRST TIME, I THOUGHT OF BREEDING TAME CREATURES, SO THAT I MIGHT HAVE FOOD WHEN MY POWDER AND SHOT WAS SPENT. THEN MY THOUGHTS TURNED TO THE IDEA OF MAKING A GARDEN. BUT WHAT COULD I PLANT?

Jan. 3. I IMPROVISED MY FENCE. I RESOLVED TO PUT TURF ON THE OUTSIDE, SO THAT ANY PEOPLE, IF THEY CAME TO SHORE, WOULD NOT PERCEIVE MY HABITATION.

Apr. 14. I HAD FINISHED MY WALL AND I NOTICED SOME FRESH GREEN SPROUTS TO ONE SIDE OF MY HABITATION. THEY WERE GROWN PERFECTLY LIKE ENGLISH BARLEY! I THOUGHT THAT GOD HAD WROUGHT A MIRACLE IN THIS WILD PLACE! THAT HE HAD SHOWN ME THAT I MIGHT GROW GRAIN!

Apr. 15. BEING AT A LOSS FOR CANDLES, I HAD BEEN OBLIGED TO GO TO BED AT DARK, NO MATTER THE HOUR. I NOW MADE A LAMP OF A CLAY DISH, GOAT'S TALLOW, AND A WICK OF OAKUM.

I COULD NOW WRITE MY JOURNAL AND READ A LITTLE AT DAY'S END.

May 1. THE SHIP WAS STRANGELY REMOVED AND CLOSER TO THE SHORE. THE FORECASTLE WAS HEAVED UP AND THE STERN WAS BROKEN AND CAST ASIDE.

I RESOLVED TO PULL EVERYTHING TO PIECES THAT I COULD, OF THE SHIP.

May 3 to June 15. I WENT EVERY DAY TO THE SHIP AND GOT A GREAT DEAL OF LUMBER AS WELL AS IRON WORK.

I CAPTURED A LARGE TURTLE OR TORTOISE, THE FIRST I HAD FOUND.

HAVING EATEN NO FLESH SINCE I LANDED IN THIS PLACE, THE TURTLE MEAT SEEMED THE MOST SAVORY I HAD EVER TASTED.

June 19. AFTER A RAIN, I FELT ILL AND WAS SHIVERING AS IF THE WEATHER WERE COLD.

June 20. NO REST ALL NIGHT, PAINS IN MY HEAD, FEVERISH.
June 21. VERY ILL AND FRIGHTENED. PRAYED TO GOD. MY THOUGHTS CONFUSED.
June 22. VERY WEAK.
June 23. A LITTLE BETTER.
June 24. SHIVERING, HEADACHE.
June 25. SWEATS.

June 27. A-BED ALL DAY, NEITHER ATE NOR DRANK. FITS AND SLEEPING. I WOKE VERY THIRSTY BUT HAD NO WATER.

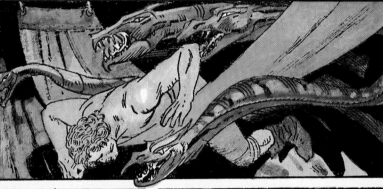

FITFULLY SLEEPING AND WAKING, MY HEAD ACHED WITH THOUGHTS OF MY SEAFARING WICKEDNESS, MY PROFANITY, MY NEGLECT OF GOD, MY STUPIDITY OF SOUL, HAVING NO FEAR OF GOD IN MY DANGER, NO THANKFULNESS IN MY DELIVERANCE. I THOUGHT TOO, OF MY REBELLION AGAINST MY FATHER, MY FAILURE OF REMORSE... SLEEPING AGAIN, I HAD TERRIBLE DREAMS.

I SAW A MAN DESCEND FROM A BLACK CLOUD IN A FLAME OF FIRE; HIS FACE WAS INEXPRESSIBLY DREADFUL; HE CARRIED A LONG SPEAR TO DESTROY ME... HE SPOKE IN A TERRIBLE VOICE: NOTHING HAS BROUGHT THEE TO REPENTANCE; NOW THOU SHALT DIE!

June 29. AFTER A NIGHT OF SOUND SLEEP, I AWAKENED REFRESHED AND CHEERFUL.

FROM THE 4TH OF JULY TO THE 14TH, I WAS CHIEFLY EMPLOYED IN WALKING A LITTLE AT A TIME, SO AS TO GATHER STRENGTH AFTER MY FIT OF SICKNESS. ON THE 15TH OF JULY I BEGAN TO TAKE A MORE PARTICULAR SURVEY OF THE ISLAND ITSELF. ON THE CREEK BANK I FOUND PLEASANT GRASSY MEADOWS. ON THE RISING GROUNDS THERE GREW GREEN TOBACCO AND DIVERSE OTHER PLANTS WHICH I DID NOT KNOW. WITH THAT, I WENT HOME.

THE NEXT DAY, THE 16TH, I WENT FARTHER. THERE WERE MELONS ON THE GROUND AND CLUSTERS OF GRAPES WHICH HAD SPREAD OVER THE TREES AND WERE NOW JUST IN THEIR PRIME. I WAS EXCEEDINGLY GLAD OF THEM, BUT ATE OF THEM SPARINGLY, TO AVOID THE FLUX.

FARTHER ALONG, I FOUND AN ABUNDANCE OF COCOA, ORANGE, LEMON, AND LIME TREES. I DETERMINED TO ENJOY THIS DELICIOUS VALE, AS IF I WERE A LORD OF THE MANOR. INDEED, I WAS TEMPTED TO DWELL THERE. HOWEVER, I DECIDED TO BUILD A SHELTER THERE, AND TO MAINTAIN MY HABITATION AT THE SHORE.

ON THE 19TH I WENT BACK TO THE GRAPE VINES, WHERE I HAD GATHERED SEVERAL BUNCHES, BUT I WAS SURPRISED TO FIND THEM SPREAD ABOUT AND TRAMPLED AND MANY EATEN. I CONCLUDED THAT SOME WILD CREATURES HAD DONE IT, BUT WHAT THEY WERE... I KNEW NOT.

THE GRAPES! WHAT..?

I WAS NOW COME TO SEPTEMBER THE 30TH, THE UNHAPPY ANNIVERSARY OF MY LANDING; THERE WERE 365 NOTCHES ON THE POST WHERE I KEPT COUNT OF THE DAYS. I MADE EVERY SEVENTH MARK LONGER, AND KEPT THE DAY AS A SABBATH, PRAYING TO GOD AND CONFESSING MY SINS.

I HAD ACQUIRED A PARROT, AND MY INK WAS BEGINNING TO FAIL ME. I HAD TO USE IT SPARINGLY, WRITING DOWN ONLY REMARKABLE EVENTS.

I HAD SAVED THE SEED FROM THE BARLEY WHICH SPRANG UP EARLIER. I WAS NOT SURE OF THE SEASON, BUT I WAS DECIDED TO SOW A PART OF IT, THE RAINS BEING OVER AND THE SUN GOING NORTH.

ON A JOURNEY THE NEXT DAY, MY DOG SURPRISED A YOUNG GOAT.

I SAVED IT ALIVE, AND CARRIED IT HOME, WITH THE DESIGN OF RAISING A BREED OF TAME GOATS.

I DETERMINED TO MAKE A BOAT, AND WORKED AT IT WITH MUCH DETERMINATION AND HARD LABOR FOR MORE THAN TWO MONTHS.

I WAS DELIGHTED WITH THE RESULTS OF MY WORK ON THE BOAT, BUT THEN I FOUND, TO MY GREAT DISMAY, THAT I COULD NOT GET IT DOWN FROM THE WOODS TO THE WATER. THIS LED ME TO REFLECT ON THE FOLLY OF BEGINNING A WORK BEFORE COUNTING THE COST.

IT CAME TO MY THOUGHTS THAT I HAD BEEN ON THE ISLAND MORE THAN FOUR YEARS, I REFLECTED AS WELL THAT I WAS MASTER OF THE ISLAND AND ALL ITS NATURAL RICHES, AND THAT PROVIDENCE HAD ALLOWED ME TO SURVIVE MY EARLY DAYS ON THE ISLAND BY MEANS OF THE PROVISIONS FROM THE SHIP.

BUT MUCH OF WHAT I HAD SAVED FROM THE SHIP WAS NOW USED UP. AND, ALTHOUGH MY CLOTHES HAD BEGUN TO DECAY MIGHTILY AFTER 4 YEARS IN THE TROPIC CLIME, I DARED NOT GO NAKED IN THE BLISTERING HEAT OF THE SUN.

I HAD SAVED THE SKINS OF THE ANIMALS AND I SOUGHT NOW TO MAKE A CAP AND CLOTHES OF THEM. I SPENT A GREAT DEAL OF TIME AND PAINS TO MAKE AN UMBRELLA, AGAINST THE RAINS AS WELL AS THE HEAT OF THE DAY.

I WAS NOW A HAIRY FELLOW INDEED.

I HAD BEEN ON MY ISLAND FIVE YEARS. I NOW HAD A HERD OF GOATS, A CROP OF GRAIN, AND A SUPPLY OF RAISINS.

I HAD FINISHED A SECOND CANOE, MORE MODEST IN SIZE THAN MY FAILED FIRST EFFORT.

I WAS EAGER TO SAIL ROUND THE ISLAND, BUT FIRST I MADE SEVERAL LITTLE VOYAGES NOT FAR FROM MY ANCHORAGE IN THE CREEK.

ON THE SIXTH OF NOVEMBER OF THE SIXTH YEAR OF MY REIGN, OR CAPTIVITY, I BEGAN MY VOYAGE TO CIRCLE THE ISLAND.

THE ISLAND ITSELF WAS NOT VERY LARGE, BUT WHEN I CAME TO THE EAST SIDE OF IT, I FOUND A GREAT LEDGE OF ROCK. BEYOND THAT WAS A SHOAL OF SAND, SO THAT I WOULD BE OBLIGED TO GO A GREAT WAY OUT TO SEA TO DOUBLE THE POINT.

I NEEDED TO JUDGE THE RISK I MUST TAKE.

I PERCEIVED A FURIOUS CURRENT RUNNING FROM SOUTH TO EAST ACROSS THE POINT, WHICH MIGHT CARRY MY CANOE OUT TO SEA.

THE WIND BEING PRETTY FRESH, I LAY HERE FOR TWO DAYS.

THE THIRD DAY, THE WIND BEING ABATED, I VENTURED OUT.

A BOAT'S LENGTH FROM THE SHORE, I FOUND MYSELF IN A GREAT DEPTH OF WATER AND A VIOLENT CURRENT WHICH PULLED LIKE THE SLUICE OF A MILL.

I BEGAN TO GIVE MYSELF UP AS LOST, CARRIED FAR OUT TO SEA. I NOW LOOKED BACK ON MY SOLITARY ISLAND AS THE MOST PLEASANT PLACE IN THE WORLD.

ABOUT NOON, A LITTLE BREEZE SPRANG UP. HOWEVER, I WAS FAR FROM THE ISLAND, AND I HAD NO COMPASS. SO, HAD I LOST SIGHT OF LAND I COULD HAVE BEEN LOST AT SEA.

A STRONG TIDE OR EDDY CARRIED ME BACK TOWARD THE ISLAND, AND THE WIND HELPED ME STEER TO SHORE.

WHEN I WAS ON SHORE I FELL ON MY KNEES AND GAVE THANKS TO GOD FOR MY DELIVERANCE.

24

I HAD NOTICED A CONVENIENT HARBOR A LITTLE WESTWARD FROM MY LANDING, AND I DECIDED TO GO ON FOOT TO VIEW THIS PART OF THE LAND.

BY A DIFFERENT WAY I NOW CAME UPON THE LITTLE CAMP WHICH I HAD MADE IN THE FRUIT LADEN VALLEY; SEEING IT GAVE ME THE NOTION TO HAVE A REST.

I LAID ME DOWN IN THE SHADE, AND FELL ASLEEP. BUT JUDGE MY SURPRISE WHEN I HEARD A VOICE CALLING ME!

ROBIN! WHERE HAVE YOU BEEN? WHY AM I HERE? POOR ROBIN CRUSOE! AWK! AWK!

I WAS AMAZED THAT MY POLL PARROT HAD COME TO THIS PLACE, BUT I WAS HAPPY THAT HE HAD FOUND ME OUT.

I FEARED I COULD NOT SAFELY RETURN BY SEA, SO I WAS RESIGNED TO GO BY LAND.

POLL, LET US HEAD FOR HOME!

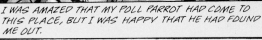

APPROACHING MY FIFTEENTH YEAR ON THE ISLAND, ONE DAY ABOUT NOON, GOING TOWARD MY BOAT, I WAS EXCEEDINGLY SURPRISED AT THE PRINT OF A MAN'S NAKED FOOT ON THE SHORE, PLAIN TO BE SEEN IN THE SAND!

I LISTENED; I LOOKED AROUND; I HEARD NOTHING AND SAW NOTHING.

I CLIMBED RISING GROUND FOR A BETTER LOOK; I WENT UP AND DOWN THE SHORE; I RETURNED TO THE FOOTPRINT.

YES, IT WAS EXACTLY A FOOTPRINT, TOES, HEELS, EVERY PART OF A FOOT! HOW IT CAME THERE I COULD NOT IMAGINE!

I RUSHED AWAY, TERRIFIED, MY THOUGHTS CONFUSED. FLEEING HOME, I WAS TERRIFIED, LOOKING BEHIND ME AT EVERY TWO OR THREE STEPS, FEARING EVERY BUSH AND TREE, AND FANCYING EVERY STUMP TO BE A CROUCHING MAN.

NEVER DID A FRIGHTENED HARE SEEK COVER WITH MORE TERROR OF MIND THAN DID I. I SLEPT NONE THAT NIGHT.

NOW I WAS FAR FROM THE FOOTPRINT WHICH HAD OCCASIONED MY FEAR, BUT FOR WEEKS AFTER, I WAS BESET BY A MULTITUDE OF APPREHENSIONS AND IMAGININGS.

AT FIRST I FANCIED THAT THE FOOTPRINT MUST BE THE DEVIL'S WORK; THEN I REASONED THAT THE DEVIL COULD HAVE FOUND AN ABUNDANCE OF OTHER WAYS TO TERRIFY ME.

I CONCLUDED THAT IT MUST BE SOME MORE DANGEROUS CREATURE.

I IMAGINED THAT BLOOD-THIRSTY SAVAGES FROM THE MAIN LAND WERE DANCING ON MY SHORES, THAT THEY HAD DESTROYED MY ENCLOSURE! I HAD THOUGHT THAT THE SIGHT OF ONE OF MY OWN SPECIES WOULD BE THE GREATEST BLESSING. NOW I TREMBLED AT THE VERY APPREHENSION OF SEEING A MAN!

I REFLECTED AGAIN AND AGAIN UPON MY FEARS. AT LAST IT SEEMED TO ME THAT IF GOD SAW FIT TO PUNISH ME, THEN EQUALLY, HE WAS ABLE TO DELIVER ME.

DURING MY 18TH YEAR ON THE ISLAND I REFLECTED THAT MY FREQUENT APPREHENSIONS ABOUT THE STRANGE PRINT OF A FOOT HAD COME TO NOTHING AND THAT I MET NO PEOPLE WHATSOEVER. MY EYES SURVEYED THE HORIZON AND SEEMED TO GLIMPSE A BOAT UPON THE SEA.

I HURRIED AGAIN TO THE HIGH GROUND, HOPING TO CATCH THE IMAGE OF THE BOAT IN MY PERSPECTIVE GLASS.

WHETHER OR NOT I HAD TRULY SPY'D SOMETHING AT SEA, IT WAS NO MORE TO BE SEEN. BUT AS I PEERED ABOUT FURTHER, AN AWFUL SCENE MET MY EYE!

I WAS CONFOUNDED! IT IS NOT POSSIBLE TO EXPRESS MY HORROR AT SEEING THE SHORE SPREAD WITH SKULLS, AND OTHER HUMAN BONES; AND I OBSERVED A PLACE WHERE THERE HAD BEEN A FIRE MADE, WHERE I SUPPOSED THE SAVAGE WRETCHES HAD SAT DOWN TO THEIR INHUMAN FEASTINGS!

I WAS SICKENED AT THE HELLISH BRUTALITY OF THE DEGENERATES WHO HAD VISITED HERE FOR THEIR HORRID PLEASURES; MY EARLIER FEAR OF DANGER WAS WASHED AWAY BY MY GRIM FLOOD OF RAGE.

I WAS SO ASTONISHED AT THE SIGHT OF THESE THINGS THAT I ENTERTAINED NO THOUGHT OF DANGER TO MYSELF.

I COULD NOT BEAR TO STAY A MOMENT. I GOT AWAY WITH ALL THE SPEED I COULD.

THERE WAS A FLOOD OF TEARS IN MY EYES, AS I GAVE THANKS TO GOD THAT I WAS DIFFERENT FROM THE DEGRADED WRETCHES WHOSE HIDEOUS WORK I HAD JUST SEEN.

HENCEFORTH I TENDED MY WEAPONS WITH GREAT CARE, BUT I FIRED THEM VERY LITTLE, BEING CAUTIOUS ABOUT THE SOUND OF A SHOT.

I NOW WENT OUT WELL ARMED, BUT I CAUGHT THE MOST OF MY WILD GAME WITH SNARES AND TRAPS.

I REMOVED MY CANOE TO A LITTLE COVE AMONG THE ROCKS, WHERE THE SAVAGES DURST NOT GO WITH THEIR BOATS FOR REASON OF THEIR IGNORANCE OF THE HARSH MIX OF CURRENTS THEREABOUTS.

AT LENGTH I FOUND A PLACE WHERE I MIGHT SECURELY WAIT AND WATCH FOR THE CANNIBALS.

NE MORNING EARLY, IN THE 25TH YEAR OF MY RESIDENCE ON THE ISLAND, FIVE CANOES CAME TO SHORE.

MAKING SURE THAT MY HEAD DID NOT SHOW ABOVE THE HILL, I RAN TO MY OBSERVATION POINT.

AS I OBSERVED WITH MY PERSPECTIVE GLASS, THERE WERE NO LESS THAN 30 SAVAGES DRAGGING TWO MISERABLE VICTIMS.

I PERCEIVED ONE PRISONER KNOCKED DOWN AND CUT APART FOR THEIR COOKERY, WHILE THE OTHER WAS LEFT STANDING TILL THEY SHOULD BE READY FOR HIM.

IN THEIR EAGERNESS TO BUTCHER THEIR VICTIM, THEY NEGLECTED TO WATCH THE OTHER...

...WHEREUPON HE LEAPED AWAY AND RAN WITH INCREDIBLE SWIFTNESS, TOWARD ME!

I WAS DREADFULLY FRIGHTENED THAT THE PRISONER WAS COMING TOWARDS ME. HOWEVER, MY SPIRITS BEGAN TO RECOVER WHEN I PERCEIVED THAT ONLY THREE SAVAGES STILL FOLLOWED HIM.

IT CAME UPON ME THAT I WAS CALLED BY PROVIDENCE TO SAVE THE PRISONER'S LIFE.

AS TO THE POOR SAVAGE WHO HAD FLED, I CALLED TO HIM, AND MADE SIGNS OF ENCOURAGEMENT.

HE KNELT, AS A TOKEN OF BEING MY SLAVE. HE SPOKE SOME WORDS WHICH I COULD NOT UNDERSTAND, BUT THEY WERE THE FIRST SOUND OF ANOTHER HUMAN'S VOICE WHICH I HAD HEARD FOR ABOVE TWENTY-FIVE YEARS!

NOW THE SAVAGE I HAD KNOCKED DOWN RECOVERED HIMSELF SO FAR AS TO SIT UP. MY SAVAGE MADE MOTIONS. I GAVE HIM MY SWORD.

MY MAN, AS I NOW THOUGHT TO CALL HIM, GRASPED THE SWORD AND RAN TOWARDS HIS ENEMY.

WHEN HE HAD DONE, HE CAME LAUGHING TO ME, IN TRIUMPH.

NOT WISHING TO REMAIN NEAR THE SHORE, NOR TO GO TO MY CASTLE, I LED THE WAY TO MY CAMP ON THE FARTHER PART OF THE ISLAND.

I GAVE HIM BREAD AND A BUNCH OF RAISINS TO EAT, AND THEN THE POOR CREATURE LAID DOWN AND WENT TO SLEEP.

HE SLEPT FOR ABOUT A HALF AN HOUR, THEN CAME TO ME WHERE I HAD BEEN MILKING MY GOATS, AND THEN KNELT AND LAID MY FOOT UPON HIS HEAD.

I GAVE HIM MILK IN AN EARTHEN POT; I LET HIM SEE ME DRINK MILK AND SOP BREAD IN IT, AND GAVE HIM A CAKE OF BREAD TO DO THE LIKE.

I TAUGHT HIM THAT I WOULD CALL HIM "FRIDAY" (WHICH WAS THE DAY I HAD SAVED HIS LIFE). LIKEWISE I TAUGHT HIM THAT "MASTER" WAS TO BE MY NAME.

WHEN WE RETURNED TO THE SHORE ON THE FOLLOWING DAY, IT WAS PLAIN THAT THE CANNIBALS WERE GONE WITH THEIR CANOES. ON THE BLOODY SAND WERE THE MANGLED AND SCORCHED LEAVINGS OF THE FEAST. I CAUSED FRIDAY TO MAKE A GREAT FIRE AND BURN THE REMAINS TO ASHES.

AT MY CASTLE, I FELL TO WORK FOR FRIDAY, ALTERING FOR HIM A PAIR OF LINEN DRAWERS, AND A JERKIN OF GOAT'S SKIN. I GAVE HIM A HARE'S SKIN CAP.

ONE FOOT APART, FRIDAY.

YES, MASTER, I DO!

I WAS GREATLY DELIGHTED WITH FRIDAY, THE MOST APT SCHOLAR THAT EVER WAS.

I TOOK FRIDAY HUNTING, THAT HE MIGHT FETCH THE GAME. I WANTED TO TEACH HIM TO PREFER ANIMAL MEAT TO HIS FORMER TASTE FOR THE HUMAN.

BUT WHEN I FIRED AT A GOAT, HE TREMBLED WITH THE FEAR THAT I HAD RESOLVED TO KILL HIM. I REASSURED HIM, BUT IT WAS SOME TIME BEFORE HE LOST HIS FEAR OF THE GUN.

FRIDAY BEGAN TO TALK PRETTY WELL. I LEARNED FROM HIM THAT THE LAND TO THE WEST AND NORTH-WEST WAS TRINIDAD AND THAT THE PASSAGE THERE BY CANOE WAS NOT DANGEROUS. BEYOND WAS A MAIN LAND, FRIDAY'S OWN, WHERE 17 WHITE MEN HAD ARRIVED IN A BOAT, DRIVEN BY A STORM.

I HAD THE IDEA OF GOING WITH FRIDAY TO THE CONTINENT WHERE I MIGHT FIND OTHER WHITE MEN. WHEN I TOLD HIM, HE THOUGHT I MEANT TO LEAVE HIM THERE. INDEED HE FETCHED A HATCHET FOR ME TO KILL HIM IF I WANTED HIM TO GO AWAY! SEEING THE TEARS IN HIS EYES, I PROMISED NEVER TO SEND HIM AWAY.

FRIDAY HAD BEEN WITH ME NOW THREE YEARS, AND I HAD BEEN ON THE ISLAND SIX AND TWENTY. WITH FRIDAY'S HELP, I HAD BEEN WORKING ON MY BOAT, SO THAT WE COULD START OUR VOYAGE.

WHAT'S THE MATTER, FRIDAY?

OH, MASTER! OH, BAD! ONE, TWO, THREE CANOE!

CAN YOU FIGHT, FRIDAY?

ME SHOOT, BUT COME GREAT NUMBER! ME DIE WHEN YOU SAY, MASTER!

THERE WERE FIVE AND TWENTY SAVAGES, THREE CANOES, AND THREE CAPTIVES, AND ONE OF THESE WAS A BEARDED WHITE-SKINNED MAN!

THE CANNIBAL PARTY HAD LANDED CLOSE TO MY CREEK, AND THIS, TOGETHER WITH MY ABHORRENCE OF THEIR BUSINESS HERE, RESOLVED ME TO ATTACK THEM.

WE CAN HIT THEM FROM HERE...

I THINK THEY SOON KILL MAN, MASTER!

I SAW PLAINLY BY MY GLASS A WHITE MAN WHO LAY THERE WITH HIS HANDS AND FEET TIED!

NOW, FRIDAY, DO AS I DO!

I DO, MASTER!

BLAM!

BLAM!

WHILST FRIDAY CONTINUED TO FIRE, I RAN TO AID THE PRISONER.

36

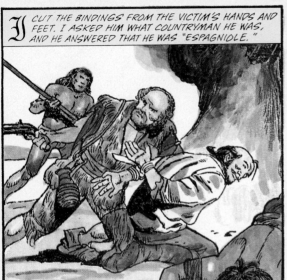

I CUT THE BINDINGS FROM THE VICTIM'S HANDS AND FEET. I ASKED HIM WHAT COUNTRYMAN HE WAS, AND HE ANSWERED THAT HE WAS "ESPAGNIOLE."

I GAVE HIM DRINK, BREAD, AND WEAPONS, AS HE TOLD ME HOW MUCH HE WAS IN DEBT TO ME. BUT I REPLIED: WE WILL TALK AFTERWARDS, BUT NOW WE MUST FIGHT!

THE WEAPONS IN HIS HANDS PUT NEW VIGOR INTO THE SPANIARD. INDEED, THE FURY OF OUR ATTACK WAS SUCH A SURPRISE THAT THEY FELL DOWN IN AMAZEMENT AND LOST THE POWER TO ESCAPE.

OUT OF FIVE AND TWENTY SAVAGES, ONLY FOUR ESCAPED AND ONE OF THEM WOUNDED.

I WAS ANXIOUS THAT THE ESCAPING SAVAGES MIGHT COME BACK TO OUR ISLAND WITH HUNDREDS MORE. RUNNING TO THE CANOE, I SEIZED IT AND WAS SURPRISED TO FIND ANOTHER POOR CREATURE CAPTIVE.

AFTER THEM, FRIDAY!

FRIDAY KISSED AND EMBRACED THE OLD NATIVE AND MADE A HUNDRED OTHER GESTURES, WHEN HE COULD FIND WORDS, HE TOLD ME: THIS WAS HIS FATHER!

MY FATHER SAY YOU KING FOR HIM, MASTER.

EL SEÑOR CRUSOE, EL REY!

WHAT SAYS YOUR FATHER ABOUT THE CANNIBALS WHO ESCAPED?

IF NOT DIE IN STORM WIND, THEY THINK DEVILS LIVE HERE AND THEY NOT COME BACK.

THE SPANIARD MADE ME UNDERSTAND THERE WERE SIXTEEN MORE OF HIS COUNTRYMEN AS WELL AS PORTUGUESE, WHO WERE SHIPWRECKED ON THE CANNIBAL SHORE.

WHILST FRIDAY AND HIS FATHER CLEARED THE BEACH, I ASKED THE SPANIARD: WOULD THE EUROPEANS GIVE ME FIDELITY IF I RESCUED THEM?

SI, SI... PERO...

I TOLD HIM PLAINLY, THAT I FEARED TREACHERY UNDER THE MERCILESS INQUISITION. BUT THE SPANIARD SWORE TO ME THAT THESE MEN WOULD BE FOREVER GRATEFUL AND FAITHFUL. THERE WAS THE QUESTION OF FOOD FOR SO MANY.

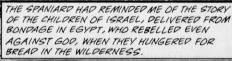

THE SPANIARD HAD REMINDED ME OF THE STORY OF THE CHILDREN OF ISRAEL, DELIVERED FROM BONDAGE IN EGYPT, WHO REBELLED EVEN AGAINST GOD, WHEN THEY HUNGERED FOR BREAD IN THE WILDERNESS.

HAVING NOW SOCIETY ENOUGH FOR SELF PROTECTION, WE WENT FREELY ABOUT THE ISLAND.

AFTER A GOOD GROWING SEASON, WE HAD AN AMPLE FOOD SUPPLY, AND I GAVE THE SPANIARD LEAVE TO GO SEEK OUT THE SHIPWRECKED EUROPEANS AND BRING THEM TO OUR ISLAND.

I HAD GIVEN THEM FIREARMS AND PROVISIONS FOR THEIR TASK. AS THEY SAILED AWAY I REFLECTED THAT IT HAD BEEN 27 YEARS SINCE I WAS DELIVERED ALONE TO THESE SHORES.

I WAS ASLEEP IN MY HUTCH ONE MORNING WHEN FRIDAY WOKE ME WITH A CALL THAT "THEY HAD COME." EXPECTING THE RETURN OF OUR VOYAGERS I TURNED MY EYES TO THE SEA. I SAW A BOAT, BUT NOT COMING FROM THE EXPECTED DIRECTION.

A BIG BOAT, MASTER!

A BOAT AND A SHIP, FRIDAY!

I DISCOVERED IT WAS PLAINLY AN ENGLISH SHIP, BUT MY MIND WAS IN CONFUSION BETWEEN JOY AND TROUBLING DOUBT.

LET NO MAN DESPISE HIS SECRET HINTS OF DANGER: WHAT BUSINESS HAD AN ENGLISH SHIP IN THIS PART OF THE WORLD, WHERE THEY HAD NO TRAFFIC? AND, THERE HAD BEEN NO STORMS TO DRIVE THEM HERE.

FRIDAY THOUGHT THE ENGLISHMEN MIGHT EAT THEIR CAPTIVES, BUT I TOLD HIM NO, THEY WILL MURDER THEM, NOT EAT THEM.

DRUNK FROM BRANDY, THE CREWMEN WANDERED OFF, LEAVING THEIR PRISONERS AT LIBERTY.

THEY WERE CONFOUNDED WHEN THEY SAW ME, HEAVILY ARMED, WITH MY GOAT'S SKIN COAT AND CAP.

GENTLEMEN! YOU MAY HAVE A FRIEND!

SENT FROM HEAVEN, THEN!

WHAT IS YOUR CASE? WHAT HAS HAPPENED?

MY STORY IS LONG, BUT IN SHORT, SIR, I WAS THE COMMANDER OF THAT SHIP BEFORE MY MEN MUTINIED...

I LED THE THREE ENGLISHMEN TO MY DWELLING.

SIR, IF I VENTURE UPON YOUR DELIVERANCE, WILL YOU THEN BE COMMANDED BY ME, AND IF YOUR SHIP BE RECOVERED, WILL YOU CARRY ME TO ENGLAND?

I WILL, AND MOST HAPPILY!

WE MUST PLAN AN ATTACK!

I SHOULD GO IN FRONT, SIR, FOR I KNOW THE CHARACTER OF THE MEN.

THE CAPTAIN WAS LOATHE TO FIRE UPON ALL THE MEN, ONLY THE TWO WHO WERE INCORRIGIBLE. WITH THAT PLAN, WE STARTED A SEARCH.

IN A FEW MINUTES WE CAME UPON TWO OF THE MUTINEERS.

HELP ME!

'TIS TOO LATE! CALL ON GOD TO FORGIVE YOUR VILLAINY!

YE MEN, IF YE BE SINCERE, I MAY SPARE YE!

THUS FAR, OUR VICTORY WAS COMPLETE.

AFTER FRUITLESS SIGNALS, THE SHIP HAD SENT ANOTHER BOAT. WE SAW THAT THERE WERE NO LESS THAN TEN ARMED MEN COMING.

BOOM

W E HAD A FULL VIEW OF THE MUTINEERS. THE CAPTAIN POINTED OUT AMONGST THEM THREE HONEST FELLOWS, THE REST BEING DESPERATE TYPES LED BY THE BOATSWAIN.

MEN IN OUR CIRCUMSTANCES ARE PAST FEAR, SIR!

IS NOT WHICH-EVER CONSEQUENCE, LIFE OR DEATH, A DELIVERANCE?

THE ARRIVALS WERE MUCH ASTONISHED HEARING NO REPLY FROM THEIR COMRADES; THEY SPLIT THEIR PARTY SO THAT THREE STAYED WITH THE BOAT AND THE OTHERS WENT OUT TO SEARCH.

HALLOO.

NOW WE WERE AT A LOSS WHAT TO DO; SEIZING THOSE ON SHORE WOULD NOT BE AN ADVANTAGE IF THOSE IN THE BOAT REACHED THE SHIP AND SAILED AWAY! WE HAD TO LURE THE BOAT BACK AND CAPTURE IT.

FRIDAY AND THE MATE ATTRACTED THE MAIN BODY OF MUTINEERS TO THE CREEK. THERE THEY WERE STOPPED, THE WATER BEING HIGH.

HALLOO!

HALLOO!

YOU! RUN AND HAIL THE BOAT SO WE CAN CROSS!

OUR TRAP WAS CLOSING.

WHEN THEY HAD SET THEMSELVES OVER, THEY LEFT ONLY TWO AT THE BOAT. THIS WAS WHAT I HAD WISHED FOR! WE ATTACKED!

NOW WE HAD THEIR BOAT! AND WE HAD KNOCKED A HOLE IN THE ONE AT THE BEACH. THEY COULD NEITHER LEAVE THE ISLAND NOR REACH THE SHIP.

IT WAS DONE IN AN INSTANT.

WHAT THE DEVIL?

YOU'RE SURROUNDED! SURRENDER NOW OR YOU ALL DIE! NOW!

THEY YIELDED.

THE PLAN WAS FOR THE CAPTAIN AND ELEVEN FAITHFUL MEN TO CAPTURE THE SHIP BY FORCE.

YE'LL HOLD THE BAD ONES HERE FOR ME, EH, GOVERNOR?

THAT WE SHALL, SIR, AND WE'LL SEE YOU SOON!

FROM ACROSS THE WATER, I HEARD THE SOUND OF GUNS.

SEVEN GUNS! THE SIGNAL OF VICTORY FROM THE CAPTAIN!

BOOM!

BOOM!

WHEN I TOOK LEAVE OF MY ISLAND, ALONG WITH FRIDAY, I CARRIED ON BOARD FOR RELIQUES THE GREAT GOAT'S SKIN CAP, MY UMBRELLA, AND MY PARROT. ALSO I FORGOT NOT MY MONEY, SO LONG UNUSED THAT IT WAS GROWN TARNISHED.

AS FOR THE NEW INHABITANTS OF MY ISLAND, I ALLOWED TO REMAIN THERE THOSE OF THE MUTINEERS WHO MIGHT BE HANGED IF THEY RETURNED TO ENGLAND. I GAVE THEM SEEDS AND FIREARMS, AND MADE THEM PROMISE TO TREAT FAIRLY WITH THE SEVENTEEN SPANIARDS EXPECTED TO ARRIVE FROM THE MAIN LAND.

WILL YE MISS YOUR LIFE ON THIS ISLAND, GOVERNOR?

THAT I WILL, SIR, FOR HOW MANY MEN HAVE MADE THEIR OWN REALM AND DOMINION, AND HAD BEEN KING OF IT FOR EIGHT AND TWENTY YEARS?

AND THUS I LEFT THE ISLAND, ON THE NINETEENTH DAY OF DECEMBER, AS I FOUND BY THE SHIP'S ACCOUNT, IN THE YEAR 1686. ON THE SAME VESSEL, AFTER A LONG VOYAGE, I ARRIVED IN ENGLAND THE ELEVENTH OF JUNE, IN THE YEAR 1687. I HAD BEEN FIVE AND THIRTY YEARS ABSENT. I DID NOT KNOW, AT THAT TIME, WHETHER I MIGHT AGAIN SEE THE ISLAND. I DID, YES, BUT THAT IS ANOTHER SURPRISING TALE.

END

Daniel Defoe was born in London in 1660, the son of James Foe, a butcher (he added the "De" prefix to his surname sometime around 1700 to assume a more genteel origin). He was educated at Stoke Newington Academy, a school set up for Dissenters from the Church of England, and studied for the ministry. However, the world of commerce fascinated him, and by the time he married in 1683, he was a hosiery merchant. Throughout his life Defoe was involved in various ill-conceived business ventures that ultimately failed, such as a scheme to sell maritime insurance during wartime, and economic matters were a mainstay of *The Review*, a newspaper he edited from 1704-1713. His first great success as a writer came with *The True-Born Englishman*, a satirical poem that supported England's German-born king. He thereafter became a prolific pamphleteer, producing more than 250 pamphlets at a time when they were socially important publications. Defoe's predilection for irony got him in trouble on a number of occasions, most notably when he was arrested and pilloried after publication of *The Shortest Way with the Dissenters*, a mock argument that lampooned religious intolerance by calling for the suppression of all Dissenters. The experience seems not to have taught him a lesson, as he used the same style for *Reasons Against the Succession of the House of Hanover* (1712); it satirized objections to the royal family by pretending to agree with the monarch's enemies, but the authorities missed the point and Defoe was arrested for treason. Defoe was active in politics, serving for a time as an undercover agent for the Tories, but his frequent changes of party affiliation earned him the reputation as a pen for hire. He was a widely travelled man, and his three-volume *A Tour Thro' the Whole Island of Great Britain* (1724-1727) was highly regarded. Defoe had turned to fiction in 1706 and wrote the first modern English ghost story, *A True Relation of the Apparition of One Mrs. Veal*, but it was not until he was almost 60 that he turned to the form in earnest. Among the slew of novels that followed were *Robinson Crusoe* (1719), his most important book; *Moll Flanders* (1722); *A Journal of the Plague Year* (1722); and *Roxana* (1724). He continued to write both fiction and non-fiction until his death in 1731, by which time he had over 560 publications to his credit.

Sam Wray was born in Iowa in 1920. He studied creative writing at the University of California at Irvine, and then worked for some years as a governmental reports writer. Wray has contributed writing and artwork to such publications as *Comics Review*, *Overload*, and *Scat*.

Pat Boyette was born in San Antonio, Texas, in 1923. He was on radio as a child actor at eight; at 16, he was a staff announcer and newscaster. Following military service in World War II, he worked in the new medium of television as a news director and anchorman for KEYL/KENS-TV, San Antonio. Boyette also worked in film, directing documentaries, educational features, and four theatrical films. He has experience as a television storyboard artist and as an advertising designer. Boyette entered comics illustration through newspaper syndicates; his work has appeared in a wide variety of publications, and has won him a prestigious Inkpot Award. Boyette painted the cover for the *Classics Illustrated* version of *The Count of Monte Cristo*, and wrote and illustrated the adaptation of *Treasure Island*.